THE HAPPY RAG

Tony Ross

RED FOX

Gregory had a rag that made him feel happy.

He called it his happy rag.

THE HAPPY RAG

A Red Fox Book

Published by Random House Children's Books
20 Vauxhall Bridge Road, London SW1V 2SA

A division of Random House UK Ltd
London Melbourne Sydney Auckland
Johannesburg and agencies throughout the world

First published by Andersen Press Ltd 1990

Red Fox edition 1992
5 7 9 10 8 6 4

Copyright © Tony Ross 1990

Printed in China

RANDOM HOUSE UK Limited Reg. No. 954009

ISBN 0 09 978080 1

Although Gregory wasn't afraid of the dark,

he was even less afraid of it when he had his happy rag.

"You shouldn't go out with that yucky old rag!"

It makes you look silly," said awful Aunt Maggie.

"It isn't a yucky old rag," said Gregory. "It's a spaceship."

And he zoomed out to play in the stars.

"You shouldn't put that dirty old thing in your mouth.

It's bad for you and your nose may fall off," said Grandpa.

"It's not a dirty old thing!" said Gregory. "It's a pirate ship."

And he sailed south to the Spanish Main.

"Don't you think you are a bit old for a gooey old blanket?

Only babies have those," said Uncle Sid.

"It's not a gooey old blanket. It's a suit of armour,"

said Gregory, waving his sword at a dragon.

When the dragon was dead

Gregory went for a walk in the park.

Suddenly, around a corner, he heard a terrible noise.

"Wooooooooohh!" it went. "Yeeeeeeeeerr!" went Gregory.

"It must be something terrible,"

I'd better be off ...

cried Gregory. "Yeeeeeeeeeerr!HELP!

... on my magic carpet."

on a wonderful flying carpet.

from the claws of a big growly bear.

And the bear chased away a magician

cried Lucy. "Wooooooooohh! HELP!"

went her big growly bear.

"It must be something dreadful,"

"Grrrrrrrr! Grrrrrrrr!"

Suddenly, around a corner she heard a dreadful noise.

"Yeeeeeeeeerr!" it went. "Wooooooooo!" went Lucy.

So Lucy took her big growly bear to the park

where nobody would put him into the washing machine.

"No!" said Lucy.

"It's the big growly bear who looks after me."

Once, Mum tried to take her rag away.

"It's ready for the wash!" she said.

But Lucy took it back again.

"It's the big growly bear who looks after me," she said.

Once, Dad took her rag away

and threw it in the dustbin. ("Dirty old thing," he said.)

Her happy rag looked after her all the time,

even when she was asleep.

Then one day, Lucy found a happy rag,

and then she felt safe.

... dark shadows and things on T.V.

... that she just had to watch.

Lucy was afraid of nearly everything.

Spiders in the bath ...

THE HAPPY RAG

Tony Ross

RED FOX

A Red Fox Book

Published by Random House Children's Books
20 Vauxhall Bridge Road, London SW1V 2SA

A division of Random House UK Ltd
London Melbourne Sydney Auckland
Johannesburg and agencies throughout the world

First published by Andersen Press Ltd 1990

Red Fox edition 1992

5 7 9 10 8 6 4

Copyright © Tony Ross 1990

Printed in China

RANDOM HOUSE UK Limited Reg. No. 954009

ISBN 0 09 978080 1

...turned on or before ... below

P1-3

THE HAPPY RAG